BEAST IN THE WOODS
FILTHY RICH LOVE

SADIE KING

LET'S BE BESTIES!

A few times a month I send out an email with new releases, special deals and sneak peeks of what I'm working on. If you want to get on the list I'd love to meet you!

When you join you'll get access to all my bonus content which includes a couple of free short and steamy romances plus bonus scenes for selected books.

Sign up here:
authorsadieking.com/bonus-scenes

BEAST IN THE WOODS

A billionaire with a bad reputation and a curvy girl that's all innocence...

Lucas

My fortune was built on taking what I want when I want it.

When I meet the wide-eyed Mya she seems like an easy victory. I'm drawn to her innocence and her curvy body. But she's woken something deep inside me, something primal, something that would ruin her innocence without thinking twice.

It breaks my heart to push her away, but she deserves better than a beast like me.

Mya

Since I became legal guardian of my little sister three years ago, she's caused me nothing but stress. Now that she's a rebellious teenager, I'm forever running around after her trying to keep her out of trouble.

Then I meet the mysterious heir to the Bancroft fortune with the wicked reputation, and suddenly I'm the one being led astray.

Beast in the Woods is a short and steamy romance featuring an alpha male and curvy younger woman.

Copyright © 2019 by Sadie King.

All rights reserved.

No part of this book may be reproduced in any form or by any electronic or mechanical means, including information storage and retrieval systems, without written permission from the author, except for the use of brief quotations in a book review.

Cover designed by Cormer Covers.

This is a work of fiction. Any resemblance to actual events, companies, locales or persons living or dead, are entirely coincidental.

www.authorsadieking.com

1

MYA

The mansion towers menacingly against a darkening sky. The dense trees from the wood surrounding it cast black shadows across the moonlit lawn. There's a faint light in one of the upstairs windows, muted by a half-drawn curtain.

A shiver runs through me, and I pull my cardigan closed. It catches on the cat's tail I've got pinned to the back of my uniform, so it doesn't quite close around my chest.

My footsteps clack angrily on the pavement, the only sound in the deserted street, as I pass the black wrought iron fence that runs around the property. Intricate patterns with spiderwebs growing between the swirls adorn the fence, and I've often stopped to admire them and wonder who lives in such a lonely looking place.

But tonight my thoughts are consumed by my sister. She's somehow managed to pick up a gig tonight, waitressing at a private party on the edge of town. If she thinks I'm letting her go out alone to a stranger's house on Halloween in the middle of nowhere, she's crazy.

I've finished my shift at the diner early so I can go with her and make sure she doesn't get herself into any more trouble.

I'm so consumed by thoughts of my rebellious little sister that I don't notice the shadow moving by the gated grand entrance to the mansion's grounds.

A demon jumps out from behind a pillar.

My heart leaps into my throat pulling a scream from my chest. The demon bursts into laughter and high fives a zombie lurking by the gate.

"Good one, dude," he says to his friend.

"Stupid trick or treaters," I say under my breath. But I can't help but smile; it serves me right for walking alone on Halloween.

I go to step around the boys, but the one dressed as a demon blocks my path.

"Hey, Cat Girl, want to stick around and help us play a trick?"

"Not really," I eye him warily.

"We've been ringing this gate for ten minutes, and no one's answered."

"Maybe they're not home," I say.

"This guy's always home," says the zombie. "He just likes to live in the dark."

I raise my eyebrows at him skeptically.

"My mom used to be his cleaner," he continues. "She

BEAST IN THE WOODS

never saw him. Never spoke to him, never even knew his name."

"So how did she know he was home?" I don't know why I'm wasting my time humoring him but I've always been curious about the mysterious owner of the mansion I walk past every day to and from work.

"She used to hear him howling."

My skin prickles, and I pull my cardigan around me again. "That's just a silly story,"

"Are you calling my mom a liar?"

"No," I say warily. "But what kind of a man howls? It's not very likely, is it?"

"Maybe he's not really a man?" says the demon. "He's big, apparently, tall as one of those trees in the woods."

I roll my eyes. "This story's getting better and better."

"It's true!" protests the zombie. "My mom says so."

"I thought she never saw him?"

"She did his laundry," says the zombie angrily. "Everything in giant sizes, she said. And she did see him once walking out from the trees. Just after she'd heard howling coming from the woods."

"It could be wolves," I say.

"Nah, they all died off years ago. And another thing; there's a whole wing of the house she wasn't allowed to go in. She used to see bats flying out of the chimneys."

He reaches into his bag and pulls something out of it. "So, it looks like it's a trick for him." He launches the object in his hand, and an egg splatters onto the gate.

SADIE KING

"Hey, don't do that." I step forward and trip over his bag, grazing my knee on the pavement. The boys laugh as I pick myself up.

"Why not? The guy who lives here is obviously loaded, and he can't even spare a bit of candy for the local kids."

"You're hardly kids, are you?" It's hard to tell under the masks but judging by their builds they look like teenagers to me.

The zombie picks up another egg and aims it at me. "You rather we play a trick on you, Cat Girl?"

My heart races, but I won't let this upstart of an adolescent threaten me. I've had plenty of experience dealing with wayward teenagers.

"You can throw that egg at me if it makes you feel better, but it's not going to get you any candy."

There's a thump on the top of my head and the dull crack of an egg breaking against my skull. Gooey raw egg trickles over the band holding up my cat ears and down my hair.

The zombie doubles over laughing as the demon comes around from behind me and high fives his friend.

Teenage assholes.

"That's for calling my mom a liar," says the zombie.

I take a deep breath and casually wipe egg from my forehead.

"You'd better run along home to your mom," I say, "because she was right. I know the man who lives here too."

I fix them with what I hope is an intense stare. "You never see him during the day because he's half vampire, half wolf. He hunts at night, feeding on the blood of teenagers he finds making out in the woods."

I'm warming to my theme, and I start walking slowly toward them.

"The howling your mom heard happens every time he makes a new kill."

The boys start backing away. One of them stumbles over the lip of the pavement.

"When he can't find what he needs in the woods, he ventures into town and stalks the kids he finds out after dark. That's why these gates are so thick. They were built to contain him."

The zombie pushes up his mask, revealing a terrified face underneath. I wonder if I've gone too far, but then they turn and run.

"You'd better get home before he finds a way to get out!" I call after them.

I laugh to myself and do a little victory dance, spinning around with my hands in the air. I freeze mid-spin. Standing on the other side of the gate is a huge figure, half-man and half-beast with yellow eyes glinting out of a rugged wolf's head. For the second time tonight, I scream.

2
LUCAS

*I*t's not the usual reaction I get from women, but then I'm not usually dressed for Halloween.

I should pull off the mask and put her at ease. That would be the gentlemanly thing to do. But I'm no gentleman, and she has just been throwing eggs at my property. So I let her scream while I survey the damage.

Thankfully she calms down quickly and seems to realize I'm a man in a mask and not actually the mythical creature she was conjuring for her friends.

"What the hell are you doing sneaking around dressed like that?" she says.

"What are you doing throwing eggs at my gate?" My voice is muffled by the mask, and she has to come forward to hear me.

"I wasn't throwing eggs. Those stupid kids were the

ones throwing eggs. You're lucky I scared them off with my story."

I laugh. She actually believes it was her that scared them off and not me appearing silently behind her.

She steps into the light cast by the single lantern on the gate, and my heart stops for a moment. She's beautiful. A curvy figure with long dark hair and wide brown eyes, her face unadorned by any make-up. I can see the flaws of her skin and the natural color of her lips. It's such a pure, natural radiance that for a moment I'm struck speechless. Then I notice the egg trickling down her forehead.

"They did this to you?" I growl.

She nods. "Yup, I got egged by teenagers."

I laugh for the second time in as many minutes, which is unusual for me.

"Come inside. I'll clean you up."

I can feel her hesitation. This is probably the time to lift the mask and show her the man underneath. But there's such an innocence radiating from her that I don't want to reveal my impure self. With the mask on I can be whoever I want to be. When she sees me as I am, I'll just be a man with all my faults, and my faults are many.

I push the button, and the gates slides silently open. A glob of egg drips off the railing and splatters onto the pavement.

I hold out a hand to her. It looks big and beefy even to my eyes, but at least she can see there's no wolf fur sprouting from it.

She accepts my hand, and I let out a breath I didn't know I was holding. Her hand is small and warm in my meaty palm, and I lead her through the gate and toward the house.

"What were you doing walking on your own in the dark?" I ask.

"I didn't know there was a curfew," she says, sticking her chin out defiantly. She'd probably look quite tough if it wasn't for the egg yolk snaking down the side of her cheek.

"A young woman like you needs to be careful walking alone at night. You could run into trouble." I realize I sound like I'm lecturing her, but I suddenly feel very protective of this tough-talking young woman with the innocent eyes.

I keep her hand in mine as I stride to the house. It's warm and comforting, and she doesn't try to remove it.

The old wooden door creaks as I push it open, and I feel her hesitate again on the steps.

"You want to call someone and let them know where you are?" I ask before we go into the house. She nods and gets her phone out.

There's a sudden emptiness when she takes her hand out of mine. The lack of warmth leaving me feeling bereft.

As she taps out a message, the hair on the back of my neck starts to prickle. She's probably texting her boyfriend, some preppy college undergrad. I clench my fists and a growl escapes my throat. She looks up, startled, and I turn the growl into a cough. I don't know what's come over me. I've had my fair share of women, but none of them have made me feel this sudden animal possessiveness.

"I've let my little sister know I'll be late." She slips her phone into her pocket.

"Your sister," I say dumbly, the anger draining away immediately.

"I told her if I'm not home in fifteen minutes to send the police to your house."

She laughs nervously, and I realize how unusual it is for a girl like her to walk into the house of a stranger wearing a wolf mask. Only on Halloween. I don't know if I admire her bravery or her stupidity, but I'm not going to turn her away.

She's woken something primal inside me. I should send her home with her innocence intact. That would be the right thing to do. But when have I ever done the right thing?

I inherited a fortune built on taking what you want; it's woven into my genes. God knows I've tried to escape it, but I've accepted it now. That's who I am. What I want I take, and right now I want this woman.

3

MYA

What the hell am I doing? I ask myself for the umpteenth time as I cross the threshold into the house of a complete stranger whose face I haven't even seen.

"Come through to the kitchen," he says.

His voice is muffled by the mask, giving it a sexy rumble and causing me to lean in close when he speaks. Every time I do, I catch an earthy scent of pine trees and sweat that's making my heart race.

He might have scared me half to death, but from the moment he stepped out of the shadows and I realized he was a very tall and well-built man, and not actually a beast, my heart hasn't calmed down. Then he wrapped his big manly hand around mine, and I almost swooned. I'm not a small girl, but he made me feel tiny and delicate. It was both disconcerting and delicious.

The man leads me through to a kitchen, switching lights on as he goes. There's a slab of cured meat hanging from a hook above the kitchen island and a magnetic strip with knives stuck to it, the sharp blades glinting in the light. I wonder again what the hell I'm doing here.

But there's something about him that makes me feel safe. Like no harm could come to me when I'm with him.

"Sit down." He pulls out a rustic wooden chair, and I swish my tail aside to sit.

He pulls out a chair in front of me.

"May I?" he asks, indicating my knee. I nod, and he picks my leg up to inspect the scrape. The reaction is instant and electrifying. His hand on my knee sends a sexy shiver right through me. He's taking a long time looking at my graze, and I'm wondering if he also feels this current that's flowing between us.

"Do you wanna take the wolf mask off now?" My voice is barely a whisper.

I like to think he grins at me, but I have no way of knowing. The yellow eyes stare unblinking from above the top of the mask. God knows where he actually sees from; I think it must be the gaping mouth.

Slowly, he lifts the mask and puts it on the table.

He looks nothing like the man I imagined; he's gorgeous. Dark shaggy hair flecked with silver; deep lines trouble his brow as if he's permanently wearing a frown. His eyes are deep blue, and they rest on mine, alert and wary and full of depths, as vast as the stormy ocean whose color they resemble. They're eyes that could turn piercing and cold in an instant, and eyes

SADIE KING

that I could stare into all day wondering what it is that makes him so wary and what causes him to frown so much.

"Hi," I say. "I'm Mya." His face relaxes, and he extends a hand.

"I'm Lucas."

We shake hands, and there's no denying the tingle I'm getting every time we touch.

"We're gonna have to rinse this cut out," he says getting up from the chair.

My gaze follows him as he walks to the basin, taking in his tall frame and broad shoulders. He must be the biggest man I've ever seen. "Do you live here alone?"

"All alone."

So no one will hear me scream, I think. I must be crazy coming in here alone. But I don't feel unsafe, exactly the opposite. "It must get lonely."

He throws me a hand towel, and I wipe the egg out of my hair while he fills a bowl with water. "Not really. I have the bats for company."

"So the stories are true!"

"What stories?" he turns around, all innocence.

"Your cleaning lady is spreading the most terrible rumors about you."

"How do you know they're just rumors?" His eyebrows shoot up wickedly, and I can't tell if he's joking or not.

"She says there's an empty wing of your house that she's not allowed in."

"That's true," he says.

"And that's where you keep the bats."

"Also true. What else?"

"You like to stay in the dark."

"True."

"And you only come out at night."

"Sometimes true."

"That she hears you howling."

He bends down to get a cloth out of a cupboard.

"So how do you explain all that?" I ask.

He comes back and kneels in front of me, placing the bowl on the floor.

"It's a big house, and I don't need much space. So I shut down half of it." He dips the edge of the cloth in water. "This may hurt."

He gently lifts up my skirt, and the skin on my knees prickle under his touch. I take a sharp intake of breath. "I'll try to be gentle," he says.

I nod, letting him think it's because it hurts, but the truth is that his touch on my bare leg is sending shivers right up to my lady parts. Watching those big meaty hands gently dab the grit from the scrape on my knee is sending my body into a spin.

He dabs the cloth in the water again and continues his ministrations.

"A family of bats moved into one of the chimneys, and I let them stay. They're a thriving colony now. That's why I don't let anyone up there. Bats can be vicious if they think they're under attack."

He reaches out the other hand and lifts my skirt

slightly to get to the top of the scrape. Oh my god. There's a rush of heat between my legs.

"It doesn't look deep," he says.

I can only nod. He presses the cloth onto my leg, dabbing gently for someone so big. I wonder what it would feel like when he wasn't being so gentle. To have those big hands running all over my body, rough and urgent.

"I use energy efficient lights throughout the house which you can't often see from outside."

He presses his thumb into the flesh of my thigh, and his hand lingers a little too long. Oh my god, this complete stranger is fondling my knee. I should pull away; I should run out the door and never come back. But his touch feels so reassuring and right, and what I really want is for him to run that hand all the way up my thigh. As if reading my thoughts, his finger slides up my leg. I catch my breath, and I'm sure he must hear my heart hammering in my chest.

"I often stay out all night." He leans in and his look is wicked, his blue eyes sparkling with mischief. His hand slides all the way up my leg, his fingers resting on the warm flesh of my inner thigh.

"How about the howling?" My voice comes out as a whisper.

"That's something you'll have to find out for yourself." He leans all the way in, and before I know what I'm doing his lips crash into mine. They're hot and persistent, and I open my lips for him, welcoming his tongue into my mouth. His fingers graze my damp panties, causing my nerve endings to tingle, and a gush of wetness explodes out of me. He hooks a finger under my panties and pulls the fabric aside. I open my thighs for him as he brushes a finger against my wet folds.

I lean back and close my eyes letting his touch carry me away. All of a sudden there's a loud banging on the door.

4

LUCAS

I slide my hand out from under her skirt and push my hard-on down as I stand up.

The banging continues, persistent and urgent.

I stride to the door, angry at whoever has interrupted my easy victory. Another five minutes, and I would have had my dick buried in that sweet, wet pussy.

As I walk into the entryway, a muffled female voice yells from behind the door.

"You'd better open up."

I hear a groan behind me. Mya has followed me into the hall.

"It's my sister," she says.

I open the door, and an angry younger version of Mya almost pounds me on the chest with her raised fist.

"What the hell are you doing with my sister?" she asks.

The resemblance is powerful. Same eyes, same mouth, same dark hair. But the style is completely different. The sister's wearing a full face of make-up, with dark smoky eyes and bright red lips. Her hair is pulled back into a slick ponytail, and the ends are blonde as if they've been dipped in bleach. It's an artificial look, so much in contrast to Mya's naturalness. She's wearing a short leather skirt and thigh high boots. I'm sure Mya said she had a younger sister, but this girl looks old beyond her years.

"What are you doing here?" Mya asks.

"What the hell are you doing here?" counters the sister. "I got your text. What the fuck?"

"I told you I'd be home by nine."

"You told me to call the police if you weren't home by nine."

I feel a pang of disquiet that Mya took my instructions so much to heart, and that she doesn't trust me. But then again, she probably shouldn't.

"It's not nine yet," says Mya, checking her watch.

"Did you think I was gonna wait around for my sister to get murdered?"

"So you called the police?"

"Of course not. I came around here myself."

"How did you get in?" I ask, interrupting the siblings' spat. But I'm genuinely curious as to how this upstart of a little sister broke into my property.

"I climbed the fence," she says, as if it's the most obvious thing in the world.

"I must remember to get a security check,"

SADIE KING

She folds her arms and eyes me suspiciously. "It's time to go, Mya. We have to work, remember."

Mya steps forward. "I remember, jeez, Keep your hair on."

"You need a lift somewhere?" I'm not ready to let this curvy little cat get away from me just yet.

"I drove here," says the sister.

"You what?" says Mya. "If you get caught driving without a license again, that's it."

The sister rolls her eyes. It's obviously a lecture she's heard before.

"I mean it, Brit," continues Mya. "They could separate us; you know that, right? They could still take you away from me."

"Spare me the lecture, Mya. I'm almost eighteen. They can't do anything after that."

Mya takes a deep breath, and I can visibly see her struggling to push down her anger. After a moment she says calmly, "We'll talk about this in the car."

Brit storms off toward the road.

Mya lets out a long breath. It's obvious dealing with her bratty little sister is a regular occurrence. "Sorry you had to witness that," she says. "I'd better go." She starts off after her sister, and I follow.

"I'll open the gate for you. Unless you want to climb over?" She shakes her head and throws me a thin smile.

I can tell her mind's preoccupied. She's behaving like the parent here, and it's pulling on something deep inside me. Making me feel for this young woman and the responsibility she shouldn't have to bear.

"Are you her guardian?"

Mya nods.

"You don't have any parents?" I ask gently.

She shakes her head. "They passed away in a boating accident three years ago. It's been just the two of us ever since."

I stop in my tracks. "I'm so sorry." She walks on, her arms folded, heels clicking on the asphalt. I jog to catch up to her. "If there's anything you need. Anything at all."

She smiles at me. "Thank you. That's kind of you. But we manage fine on our own."

Something catches her eye, and she frowns. "Brit come down from there. Lucas is going to open the gate for us."

I look up in time to see her sister hoisting a leg over the top railing. She gives us a sarcastic smile and jumps down on the other side, landing heavily on her heeled feet.

Mya sighs. "Sorry," she says.

I push the button to open the gate. I could have done it from the house, but there's something about this girl. I want to spend every moment I can with her. Maybe it's her innocence I'm drawn to, or maybe it's the memory of her soft pussy against my fingertips.

She turns to go, and I reach out my arm and clasp her shoulder. She turns to face me expectantly.

"Mya..."

Beeeep

SADIE KING

Brit's in the car already and has her hand slammed down on the horn.

"All right, all right, I'm coming," says Mya, jogging across the pavement. "Sorry," she mouths to me as she gets in the car. She starts up the car, and they're about to pull away when Brit opens her door and jumps out.

"Brit!" Mya calls after her.

Brit bounds over to me.

"Stay away from my sister," she hisses. She's right up close, and I can smell cigarettes on her breath and peppermint as if she's tried to disguise the smell.

"I'm sure Mya is old enough to look after herself."

"She is. But she's not experienced with men. And I've heard all about you, Mr. Lucas Bancroft. You've got quite the reputation. Thinks he's so rich he can take what he wants. Well, not my sister. That's why I came over here to get her. You want a quick fuck, find a girl like me. But Mya's still a virgin. She's not for the likes of you."

"Brit!" Mya calls again from the car.

Before I can answer, Brit spins around and jogs back to the car.

"Keep your hair on," she says to Mya.

My mind is reeling as they pull away from the curb. I should be offended, but she's so close to the truth that it hurts. A virgin. I was about to deflower a virgin, for no other reason than that I liked the look of her innocent face.

Just one more innocent piece of the world I was

prepared to ruin for my own gain. For my own selfish desire. I slam the gate shut and saunter back to the house. Brit's right. If I want a woman, I should stick to my own kind: heartless and world weary. And I should definitely stay away from Mya.

5

MYA

"What was all that about?" I ask Brit as we pull away from the mansion.

"What was what?" She feigns innocence.

"Jumping out of the car like that?"

"I asked if he had a spare cigarette."

"Brit! I thought you'd given those up." It seems my sister is hell bent on self-destruction in all of it forms.

"He didn't have any, so you don't need to worry."

"I do worry. I worry about you constantly. You can't keep going like this; you're still a minor."

"I'm almost eighteen."

"You're not though. You're seventeen and a half. You've got six months to go until you can do what you like. But while you're still in my care, you live by my rules."

"Chill out, Mya. You're so uptight."

"I just don't want you ruining your chances of getting into a good college."

BEAST IN THE WOODS

"What if I don't want to go to college? What if I want to have some fun instead?"

It's the same argument we've been having for the last six months. I'm not letting Brit miss out on a chance of getting out of this town. She's smart, when she can be bothered.

"You're going to college. No question. I wasn't able to, but you can. It's what Mom and Dad would have wanted."

"What if it's not what I want?"

I sigh warily, too tired and flustered and gooey with egg to fight. "We're not doing this Brit, not tonight. I'm working hard for you to stay in school. Don't throw that away."

"You don't need to work so hard. You don't need to come to this job tonight."

"And leave you to go alone? To a job where they've asked for female hosts only? What's a host anyway?"

"They said we'll be waitressing."

"Yeah, well, I'm not sending you out to waitress, slash host, a private party on your own."

"It seems I'm not the one who needs a chaperone," she mutters.

"What's that supposed to mean?"

"It means, what were you doing with Lucas Bancroft anyway?"

Heat rises up my neck, and I stare straight ahead at the road. I'm still in shock that I let a complete stranger run his hands up my thighs and over my most intimate areas. And the most shocking thing is that I liked it.

No, I loved it! And if Brit hadn't shown up banging on the door, I would have let him do a whole lot more.

"You always get on me for wanting to have a good time, and now here you are letting yourself get seduced by the man with the worst reputation in town."

"I've never heard of him."

"No, you wouldn't have. But believe me, there are a lot of women who have."

I can't help but smile. "Ah little sister, you came to save my virtue?"

"Don't be a dick, Mya. I came to get you because I don't want to be late for this job."

I sigh. Of course she was only thinking about herself. She always does. It's usually me that's bailing her out of trouble.

I've been Brit's legal guardian for three years and it hasn't been easy. She went off the rails when Mom and Dad died, and she's never really found her way back. I try my best to keep her on the straight and narrow, but it's so freaking hard.

She's right though. How am I meant to set a good example by wandering into some strange man's house? I don't know what came over me. I remember his hand on my thigh, and a shiver runs through me. I shake the thought from my head. I just need Brit to stay focused for another six months, to finish school and get into a good college.

I just need to hold it together for six more months. I need to set a good example. Be the model sister, mother, and guardian all rolled into one. And that

BEAST IN THE WOODS

means staying away from strange men, no matter how sexy they are.

I take a deep breath and put on a bright smile.

"I just need to head home quickly to change, and then we're ready to go. What kind of party doesn't start 'til 10 p.m. anyway?"

Her eyes twinkle. "That, big sister, is what we're going to find out."

6

LUCAS

*I*t's after midnight when I mount the stairs of the secluded country mansion. I show my invitation to the doorman. He inspects it carefully, and then opens the door. Another man pulls aside a red velvet drape and ushers me through.

I'm assaulted by a wall of hazy smoke and incense. Fires blaze in the grates, and the chandeliers are hung with real candles. It's loud with the babble of conversation, the cackle of laughter, and the clink of champagne flutes.

Partygoers in loose interpretation of Halloween dress fill the room, overflowing up the grand staircase and into the halls.

It's already hot under the wolf mask, and the smell of candle wax and woodsmoke is making my head swim.

A waitress in a playboy bunny outfit comes past, and I grab a glass of champagne. I have to lift the mask

BEAST IN THE WOODS

to knock it back, and as it falls back into place someone grasps me by the arm.

"Lucas? I thought it was you under there." It's a woman in a black leather catsuit.

"I was hoping you'd be here tonight," she says, flashing me a seductive smile. "Although I don't know why you have to wear such a scary looking mask."

"It's Halloween," I say.

She tilts her head back and laughs as if I've just said the funniest thing in the world.

I take her hand off my arm and start to move away.

"See you upstairs later?" she calls after me.

"Maybe," I mutter.

I weave my way through a room thick with costumed partygoers. I pass a woman wearing nothing but red body paint. Her breasts are painted as two red carnations, open and full. She eyes me as I walk past, and a red hand reaches out to stroke my wolf face.

"You animal," she murmurs as I squeeze past.

I keep walking and almost trip over a man dressed as a lion on his hands and knees. A woman in a witch's cape straddles his back. Her cape hangs open, revealing a black lacy bra with peek-a-boo slits where her nipples poke through. He bucks underneath her, and she throws her head back and laughs, a high-pitched cackle like broken glass scraping together.

I push past them and almost collide with a woman in a large crinoline gown.

She shoots out a hand to steady herself. Her eyes are wide and dreamy, and she fixes them on me.

SADIE KING

"You want a turn?" she says.

I wonder what she means, but then I notice a pair of feet poking out from beneath her skirts. She follows my gaze.

"Oops." She readjusts her skirts over the feet.

She resumes eye contact with me, her smile mischievous and inviting. A gasp escapes her lips, and her mouth falls open, her eyes widening. For a moment I'm fascinated, but then an image of Mya flashes into my head. Her innocent, artless smile in comparison to this brash woman, in comparison to everyone here.

I suddenly feel an uneasiness in my stomach. I tear myself away from her gaze and head for the stairs. It's a wide open staircase with red velvet carpet. As I head up, I pass a woman in a bondage outfit leading a man by a leash attached to a leather collar around his neck. She winks at me as they go past.

Off the landing there's a wide hallway with several closed doors and a bouncer standing guard by each. I go to the first room, and he gives me a curt nod and opens the door.

It takes a while for my eyes to adjust to the dark, but I don't need to see to know what's going on. The grunts and moans are enough to let me know. I press my back to the wall, the sickness in my stomach growing.

There's the clink of metal as the man next to me undoes his belt buckle.

Suddenly I need to get out of here, to get some air. I knock twice, and the bouncer opens the door.

"You might prefer the lavender room." He nods across the hall. "Women only, but anyone can watch,"

I push past him and head back to the landing.

A waitress goes past, and I grab a glass of water and lift my mask to throw it down my throat.

I lean my palms on the banister and watch the scene in the main room below. My heart is racing, and it's not because I'm turned on, far from it. I feel a sickness in my gut like someone's twisting a blunt knife. I don't know if it's the heat, or the smells, or the champagne, or the shameless display of unchecked carnal desire and the knowledge that I'm usually at the center of it.

I think of the innocent Mya, and what she'd think of me if she knew what I really was.

I'm disgusted at myself for what I am, and for what I've done in my life.

I take a few deep breaths trying to get my heartbeat under control. I watch a waitress trying to navigate around the woman in the crinoline dress. The waitress holds the drink tray over her head, struggling to get past the wide skirts. Her outfit looks too tight for her full figure, and the ears are sliding off. She turns around, and my stomach contracts. It's her. Mya. She's trussed up in a playboy bunny outfit and her face is painted with make-up, but it's definitely her.

I race down the stairs, keeping my eyes on Mya as she crosses the room. She reaches a door, and a man in a devil outfit opens it for her and follows her through. My fists clench as I push my way through the crowd, not caring about the rude comments that follow me.

The door leads to an empty corridor with several doors leading off it. I push open the first door, and it slams open crashing against the wall. It's empty. I try the next one, and the one after that, until I find the one to the kitchen.

Mya's pushed up against a bench and the man in the devil outfit is leaning over her, one hand on her thigh. As I barge into the room they both turn to me. Her frightened expression tells me everything I need to know. In one stride I pull him off her.

"Hey, what the...?" His words are cut short by my fist connecting with his face. His nose crunches beneath my knuckles and his head jerks back, blood splattering across my tuxedo. I let him go, and he slumps against the bench and drops to the floor.

Mya's staring at the man out cold on the tiles, her mouth wide open.

"Did he hurt you?"

She shakes her head. "He was trying to touch me."

My blood pulses and I have a strong urge to kick his unmoving body, but I restrain myself. She's seen enough violence for one night.

"Are you all right?" I say tightly.

"I'm fine." She nods. "Just a little shaken."

Every instinct in me wants to take her in my arms, wrap her up and tell her she'll be okay.

Instead I pull off the wolf mask and slam it onto the bench.

"What are you doing here?" I growl out through gritted teeth. Mya doesn't belong in a place like this.

Her expression hardens. "I'm working."

"I can see that. I didn't think a place like this was your style."

"And what kind of a place is this exactly?" There's a challenge in her eyes, which is both infuriating and incredibly sexy.

"Why don't you tell me what you think is going on here?" I ask, curious to find out how much she knows.

"It's a Halloween party."

"Go on."

"But the costumes are pretty risqué, and some of the guests are..." She searches around for the right word. "...not afraid to make out in front of each other."

She's looking at me, satisfied, as if she's gotten the answer right. God she's beautiful, and so incredibly naive.

"A girl like you shouldn't be at a party like this."

"Why not? I can handle seeing a few boobs, you know." I almost smile, but her blissful ignorance is what almost got her into trouble.

"Because there's men like him," I kick the devil's leg with my foot, "who would take advantage of a girl like you."

"And what exactly is a girl like me?"

I put my arms out on either side of the bench, trapping her between them.

"Innocent, untouched."

She looks at me with those big innocent eyes. She's so fucking sexy. I lean in, my body drawn to hers.

"This isn't an ordinary Halloween party." I'm so

SADIE KING

close I can smell her lipstick and something tart, alcoholic. "Have you been drinking?" I ask.

"Only the punch," she says. "The non-alcoholic one Karl said was for the waitresses."

"Show me."

"She points to a glass bowl on a bench by the fridge. I stride over and scoop some into the ladle. One sniff tells me all I need to know, but I taste it to be sure.

"There's vodka in this."

Her eyes go wide. "Karl said it was non-alcoholic."

"Karl's an asshole. How much have you had?"

"Two glasses, I think. No, maybe three. It's hot out there."

My blood is racing. I'm angry at Karl, and at her for being so goddamn naive.

"You've got no business being at a place like this." I put my hands on either side of her again, trapping her against the bench. "Do you really not know what type of party this is?" I lean in, making her look at me. "Entry is by invitation only, and guests are invited based on their willingness to leave their inhibitions at the door."

"I had figured out that much."

"Women wear costumes they can easily shed. The fires are lit so the guests don't get cold when they undress."

She's starting to look uneasy but I press on, leaning in to her.

"People come here so strangers can look at them, touch them." I'm enjoying shocking her. Those wide eyes are making my dick hard. "Have you been upstairs?"

She shakes her head, and relief floods me.

"Upstairs there are rooms where couples have sex while partygoers watch." Her eyes go even wider. I'm so close to her now I can see the lines of makeup drawn onto her eyelids. I lean right in so I'm whispering into her ear.

"Some of the rooms are for women only. Some of them anyone can join in."

Her breath is coming short and sharp, making her breasts rise up and down.

"This isn't a Halloween party, Mya," I move my mouth down so I'm brushing her lips. "This is an orgy."

As she opens her mouth in a surprised gasp, I crash my lips down on hers. She is motionless for a second, and then she presses forwards to meet me. I dart my tongue in and claim her mouth. My hand slides up her thigh, and she trembles against me. I press my body into hers so she can feel my hard dick against her.

My body is on fire from this girl. Her kiss, her tongue in my mouth, her body pressed against mine. I want to rip this stupid bunny costume off her and take her right here on the kitchen bench, thrust my cock deep inside her virgin pussy. But something doesn't feel right.

There's a groan from the man on the floor. I pull away from Mya, and she looks at me full of disappointment and need. It takes all my self-restraint not to give her what she wants. But she's a virgin, and she's drunk.

I'll not have her wake up tomorrow full of regret. She deserves better than a man like me.

She leans in to kiss me again, and I duck my head. The shock of rejection crosses her face.

"You're drunk," I say.

"I don't care." She presses herself into me, her body rubbing against my hard-on. It's almost more than I can bear.

I grab her by the chin and lift her face up to mine. "I'm not a good man, Mya."

"I don't care. I want you."

"You don't know what you're saying." I run my hand up between her legs. It's warm and damp, and my god I want to sink into her softness.

"I could take you here, fuck you hard. Make you come and pleasure myself on you. I could take your virginity."

"Yes, I want that," she whispers.

"Then do you know what I'd do?"

Her breathing is shallow as she looks at me expectantly.

"I'd leave you here and go home. I'd never think of you again. I'd move on to the next woman. You'd just be one quick fuck at a Halloween orgy."

She pulls away from me, shocked at my change of tone. It breaks my heart, but I have to be harsh. She can't give herself to a man like me.

"I need to get home." She pushes away from me, blinking rapidly as if holding back tears. I want to punch myself for hurting her.

"I'll give you a lift." I take her arm, and she pulls away from me.

"No need. I have my car."

"You can't drive. You've been drinking."

She crosses her arms but nods at me.

"Fine, you can give me a lift, but don't talk to me. And don't you dare touch me."

Her eyes flash angrily as she pushes past me out of the kitchen. I know turning her away is the right thing to do, but my insides are churning as I watch her walk away from me.

"Where's your sister?" I ask.

"She's upstairs."

Of course the sister is upstairs. I just hope she hasn't done anything stupid.

"I'll go find her," I say. "Get your coat and wait by the door."

Mya doesn't look back as she heads to the entrance, and I head up the staircase.

"I'm looking for a waitress." I speak to the first bouncer and he smiles knowingly.

"Aren't we all."

"Dark hair with blond ends. You seen her?"

"Sure, she took some drinks into the blue room a minute ago." I start to walk away, and he calls after me. "Better go easy, buddy. Boss man's taken a liking to her."

The bouncer for the blue room opens the door and

I brace myself, not knowing what I'll find. There's a four-poster bed in the middle of the room. The posts have been converted into stripper poles and four women dance around them, demonstrating varying levels of skill.

There's a crowd gathered around the bed, some watching the dancers and some talking and laughing. I scan the room and spot a pair of bunny ears in the corner. It's Brit. She's holding a drink tray and chatting to Karl. He's the owner of the house, the organizer of this party, and a man with fewer morals than I have. Karl works for Damon Fletcher, who isn't a man you want to cross. Damon runs a criminal syndicate and controls the coast, but at heart he's a family man. He never attends Karl's party's and with two young daughters of his own I wonder what he'd think of an underage girl being here.

I stalk over to Brit just in time to see Karl slip something into her hand. She pockets it and looks up at me.

"Why aren't I surprised to see you here?" she says.

"Get your things. I'm dropping you and your sister at home."

"I'm working. I can't just leave."

"I'll pay you double. Come on, Mya's waiting."

Karl stands up. "You stealing my waitresses away, Lucas?"

"Their shift is over. They're coming with me."

"Don't be greedy. We all like a bit of sister on sister

action. I was hoping to get these two in the lavender room later."

Before he finishes talking, I've got him by the throat, and he's pinned against the wall. There're gasps from around the room and all eyes turn to us.

"You don't touch these sisters." My fingers tighten around his throat, and he makes a gurgling noise. His face is going red, but I apply more pressure.

"They don't come here again. Do you understand?" He nods. For a moment the anger courses red through my veins, and I want to crush him. But there's a room full of people watching, and Mya's waiting for me downstairs. I let him go and he slumps against the wall, gasping for air.

"That's the last time you're getting an invite," spits Karl.

"Good," I say. "I'm done with your parties."

One of the women from the poles has come over, and she's pulling up a chair for him. He bats her away.

Karl smiles. "You say that Lucas, but I've seen the beast inside you. You think you can escape this, but you'll be back, begging me to let you in. There's no escaping what you are."

I grab Brit by the hand and lead her through the crowd. She's fighting me all the way, but I keep a firm grip on her. I can't hear what she's saying to me over the noise of the party, but I catch the words "bastard" and "shithead."

We meet Mya at the entranceway. I'm relieved to see she's got her coat on, but the anger in her eyes hasn't dissipated. She's holding Brit's coat and somehow manages to coax her into it and into my car.

Mya's in the front seat with her arms folded in a stony silence while Brit swears at me from the backseat. Great. I've managed to piss off both the sisters, but at least I've gotten them out of there.

As I drive away, I feel my stomach start to unclench. I know for certain I'm never going back to one of Karl's parties.

7
MYA

I'm so furious at myself. I basically threw myself at a complete stranger. But it felt so good to kiss him. His hands on me made me want more of him, and for one stupid moment my heart wanted him too. And I almost believed he felt it too. Which just proves how naive I am when it comes to men. Or maybe it's the vodka clouding my common sense.

Which just proves that what he said was right. I almost gave myself to a man I barely know. Damn him. He must have some integrity if he didn't use me and dump me like he could have so easily.

Even now with him sitting next to me in the car, my body is hot, and I can't stop thinking about his touch. I'm willing him to reach out and put his big, rough hand on my thigh.

"Who the hell do you think you are telling us what to do?" Brit's anger pours out of the back seat.

SADIE KING

"I was having fun in there."

"Brit," I say. "Do you know what kind of party it was?"

"Enlighten us, sister." The sarcasm drips off her tongue.

"It was an orgy."

"Well, duh. Of course it was an orgy." I can almost feel her rolling her eyes at me. "What did you think was going on?"

I slump further down in my seat. Am I really so naive that I was the only one who didn't know what was going on in there?

"I wouldn't have let you go if I'd known."

"Oh Mya, grow up. It's grown-ups having a bit of fun. No big deal."

"But you're not a grown-up Brit. You're only seventeen."

"Seventeen and a half. And who are you to lecture? You picked up the biggest player at the party."

"I didn't pick him up."

Brit snorts and I glance over at Lucas. His eyes are on the road, but he's clutching the steering wheel so tight I can see the veins in his knuckles pulsing.

"It's clear the guy has a boner for you, Mya, so don't play Miss Innocent with me."

The car swerves to the side of the road and pulls over. Lucas turns to Brit in the backseat. His demeanor is calm, but that vein in his knuckle pulses double time.

"You will speak to your sister with respect."

BEAST IN THE WOODS

Brit's so shocked to be told off that her mouth hangs open.

"Mya has sacrificed a lot to look after you, and all you do is cause her stress. I don't care if you want to give yourself to every man in town. But you don't get to speak to your sister like that."

Brit slumps back into her seat and folds her arms, but she stays quiet for the rest of the drive home.

Lucas pulls back onto the road, and I steal a glance at him. He keeps his eyes on the road, but at least his veins aren't pulsing anymore.

I direct him to our house, and as soon as we pull up Brit jumps out and slams the door behind her.

Lucas finally turns to face me, his expression unreadable in the dim light. I'm not sure if it's the vodka making me lightheaded and stupid, but I can't stay angry at him. I reach out and run my hand over his cheek.

"Thank you," I say. He grabs my hand in his, and his touch is so warm it sends a thrill through me.

"Be careful," he says, his lips brushing the pulse of my wrist.

I lean in and give him a peck on the cheek. His scent fills my nostrils, and I linger with my cheek next to his.

"I'm a bad man, Mya," he says into my ear. His breath on my skin makes all my hair stand on end, but I force myself to pull back before I throw myself at him again.

"I don't think you're all bad," I say.

I get out of the car and walk to the house, my heart

pounding. It's not until I'm safely inside that I hear his car pull away.

It's a few hours later, and I'm lying in bed with the covers tangled around my legs. Moonlight pours through the curtains and straight onto my pillow. I turn over to face the wall and close my eyes. I see his face before me, turbulent blue eyes full of desire and conflict. He rejected me in the cruelest way, but I can't stop thinking about him. His touch on my thigh, the shape of his hardness pressed into me.

Heat spreads between my legs and I turn over to face the window, hot and restless. He pushed me away, but I saw the desire in him that matched my own.

I roll over again, but I can't get comfortable; my body's on fire. I get out of bed and open the window.

The streets are quiet now; the trick or treaters have long ago gone home to bed. A cool breeze catches the curtain, and as it falls, I see a shape in the shadows by the wood. I snatch up the curtain. It's a man, a tall, well-built man. My heart skips a beat. I don't know what time it is or how long he's been there, watching my window.

I go quietly down the stairs and out the back door. I know I shouldn't. He pushed me away; he's no good for me. But something is drawing me to him, something primal deep inside of me, something I can't control. I have to see him. I have to feel his lips on mine, his hands on me, whatever the consequences. I go to him.

"Mya..."

"Shhhh." I bring my finger to my lips. I don't want him to try to talk me out of what I'm about to do.

He takes me in his arms, and I press my body into him. His lips crash down on mine, and I meet his urgent kiss. I feel him getting hard through my thin nightdress.

"Are you sure?" he asks, his voice husky.

I nod.

"Come with me."

He drapes his jacket over my shoulders and takes me by the hand. He leads me into the woods. He guides me over a fallen tree trunk and into a small clearing where the moonlight breaks through the dark trees.

He pushes me against the trunk of a tree, the rough bark catching on my skin. His hand runs up and under my nightdress, pressing the soft flesh of my thigh. I gasp as he gets to my panties.

"Mya," he whispers into my neck, "I can't stop thinking about you."

His breath tickles my skin and I tilt my head back, inviting him to take more of me. His warm mouth kisses my neck, sending a rush of heat through my body. He takes the top of my night dress in his teeth, and in one pull it rips down the front. I gasp as the night air hits my breasts. Then his warm hands are on me, sliding over my breasts, running down the flesh of my stomach to cup my hips, exploring my body hungrily.

I moan as he takes my breast in his hand, my nipple hardening under his touch. The sensation running through my body is almost too much to bear. I arch my back and he leans in, taking my nipple in his mouth.

"Lucas..."

He lifts his head. "You want me to stop?"

"No, I want you to keep going."

"Good."

I reach for his belt buckle and he lifts my hands, pinning them above my head.

"Not yet, Mya. I'm going to pleasure you first."

His other hand runs over my cotton panties, damp with my need. I'm powerless under his touch, my body pulsing with desire. His hand strokes my pussy through the panties, and I cry out as he finds my clit.

His tongue flicks my nipple as his hand works faster and faster on my pussy until I can't take it anymore and I cry out, my body climaxing under his touch. He waits for my shuddering to stop, then he pulls slowly away. I feel a sudden coldness at the loss of his touch. He must see it in my face, because he chuckles softly.

"Don't worry, Mya. I'm not finished with you yet."

8

LUCAS

$\mathcal{I}$ drop to my knees. Her nightdress hangs open before me, revealing white cotton panties wet with her juices. I hook my thumbs over the fabric and slide them down her legs. She steps out of them, and I nudge her legs apart and bury my head between her thighs.

Her pussy tastes sweet and earthy and like everything good. She moans when I find her clit. I lick her softly and slowly, savoring her taste. I slide a finger into her slit. She's tight and wet, and my dick's aching to be inside her. She runs her fingers through my hair, pulling my face into her. I pick up the pace and she explodes over my tongue, her sweet taste filling my mouth. Her cries echo through the woods, and it's like a calling card for my dick. I can't hold off any longer. I have to be inside her.

I run my hands up her body, over the soft folds of her stomach to her full breasts. I have to touch every part of her, to make her mine. She fumbles as she undoes my belt. Her inexperience makes my blood race and I know I should take it slow, but the animal inside of me is raging to claim what's mine. I bat her hands away and ease my aching dick out.

Her eyes widen as she sees my girth.

"Don't worry, Mya." I place her hand on my dick, and she wraps her fingers around me. "Your pussy was made for me."

"Will it hurt?" she whispers as her hand slides down my shaft.

"Yes," I moan. "It will hurt." Her hand stops, but I'm not going to lie to her. I lean in so I'm whispering into her ear. "It will hurt when I first fuck you. But only for a moment, when I break through your virgin barrier."

Her hand starts moving again, up and down my shaft. "I wish I could tell you I'll be gentle. But the truth is I'm going to fuck you hard and fast. I need you, Mya. I can't explain it, but I need to fuck you, to possess you." Her breasts are bouncing up and down with her shallow breathing, and I can't hold back any longer. I run my hands down to her hips and flip her around so she's facing the tree trunk.

She gasps in surprise but doesn't resist.

"Bend over and put your hands on the tree," I tell her.

She does as she's told, and I lift her nightdress, exposing her bare ass. Nudging her legs apart I move forward, running my cock over her pink asshole and down to her soft wet folds.

My heart's hammering in my chest, and my dick's dripping with pre-cum and pussy juice. I push the tip in, and it's like an electric shock running through my body. She's so tight, but I have to have more. I grab her breasts in my hands and push forward. She cries out, and I halt as I feel her virgin wall. It takes everything I have to pause.

"You ready, Mya?" I pant.

"Yes," she whimpers.

I thrust forward, breaking through her virginity and claiming her cunt. She cries out, and I howl with her. She's squeezing my dick in a clammy wetness that makes my whole body throb. I ease myself out and thrust again and again until her cries turn to moans. One hand holds the flesh of her ass and the other cups a breast as I pound her hard against the trunk of the tree.

Her hand slides down to rub her clit, and her fingertips graze my balls as they slap against her. It almost sends me over the edge. My blood is thundering in my ears, and all my senses are concentrated on the sensation of my dick sliding into her tight pussy.

The beast inside me has taken over, and as my climax builds my fucking becomes more urgent. She cries out with every thrust until I feel her pussy contract, and it sends me over the edge. I shoot my seed deep inside her as I howl out my orgasm, the sound echoing through the forest and into the night. She howls with me, two animals calling out their pleasure.

SADIE KING

I stay inside her until the shuddering stops. Then I ease out and turn her around and pull her close to me. She's trembling still, and I pick up my fallen jacket and wrap it around her.

"You okay?"

She nods. "I feel sleepy."

"You can sleep here. I'll keep you safe."

I lay down on a patch of fallen leaves and pull her into me.

"Aren't there wolves in the woods here?" her eyes are droopy, and she's almost asleep.

"I'm the worst beast in the woods you'll come across tonight," I tell her.

She smiles, and I kiss her forehead. Her eyes close, and I watch her for a while in the half moonlight. She's so pure and beautiful and full of goodness. Watching her makes me feel like maybe I don't have to be the man people think I am. Maybe I could be a better man.

It's been a long time since I last lay with a woman like this, and I fall asleep easily with the warmth of her body pressed against mine.

9

MYA

I wake up to the sound of a twig snapping. For a moment I don't know where I am. Then I feel the dull ache between my legs and his heavy arm draped over me.

I open my eyes. A crow is watching me from a tree opposite. It tilts its head, one beady eye looking at me as if to say, "I know what you did last night."

The memories of Lucas send heat creeping up my neck. I smile to myself. It was good; it was better than I ever hoped it could be. The smile fades on my lips as I remember his words from the party. That he'd take me, then never think of me again.

I carefully lift his arm and roll out from under him. He stays sleeping as I replace his arm by his side. He looks peaceful as he sleeps. The deep worry lines from yesterday have faded, and he looks almost happy.

For a moment I think about staying, crawling back into his arms. He said those things at the party, but last night I felt sure we had a deeper connection. He fell asleep holding me; surely that means something. But then what do I know about men? If there's one thing I've learned in the last twenty-four hours, it's how incredibly naive I am. I'm not going to stick around to wait for him to leave me.

My nightdress is torn, and I don't know where my underwear is. I wrap his coat around me, I'm sure he won't begrudge me taking it, and set off in the direction I think is home. I'm barefoot, wearing no underwear, and in a torn nightie. The ultimate walk of shame. Only I've never felt happier or more alive.

I'm humming to myself as I come out of the woods and into our backyard. The house is still and quiet and I tread carefully to the back door, hoping I can get inside without waking Brit.

The door is locked, which is weird because I'm sure in my lust-driven state I came out without locking it. I reach under the loose brick to get the spare. I let myself in quietly and sneak upstairs.

There's no noise from Brit's room, so I head straight to the bathroom for a hot shower. As the water warms me up and I return to reality, the full realization of what I've done hits me. We didn't even use protection. In our haste to get it on, I let a man with a wicked reputation have sex with me with no protection. How could I be so stupid? Getting pregnant by a guy that doesn't want to see me again is the last thing I need. I'm going to have to tell Brit. She'll rant and rave at me, but she'll know what I need to do.

I wrap myself in a towel and knock softly on her door.

"Brit?" There's no answer. I knock again and turn the handle.

"Brit, you awake?"

Her bed is empty. I throw back the door and yank open the curtains. Her closet is open and half empty. Her bed looks like it hasn't been slept in, and there's a note on the pillow. I snatch it up.

Mya,

I can't live the life you want me to. Don't worry about me. I can look after myself.

Brit.

Panic rises in my chest.

"Brit!" I fly through the house calling her name, but I already know she's gone. I throw on some clothes and grab my car keys before I remember I left the car at the party, or orgy, or whatever it was.

Damn, the taxi out there is going to cost me almost a week's wages. For a moment I think of calling Lucas, but the last thing he wants is last night's lay asking for a ride all over town.

I find a taxi number and pace the house while I wait.

SADIE KING

I start calling her friends, but no one's answering at this time in the morning. I'll drive around to every single one of their houses and bang on the door 'til they answer.

I'm trembling by the time the taxi arrives. I can't shake this sense of foreboding and guilt. Like it's my fault for following my selfish desires instead of being here for my sister. I sink into the back seat of the taxi.

Lucas was right. All I feel about last night is regret.

10

LUCAS

I wake up feeling cold and damp, and I know before I open my eyes that she's gone.

She's taken my jacket which is a relief, but I'm not sure she even knows the way home. I set off after her. I know these woods well. They're practically my own backyard.

It's prime land on the outskirts of a growing town. The developers have had their eyes on them for years. My father was the one that started clearing the woods. He built shopping malls, industrial areas, and created new residential suburbs. He made a fortune. I inherited it, and I've been trying to repair the damage ever since.

Now I buy up the land. I own most of the woods here now. I've been offered millions to sell it. But what do I want with more money? It can't fill this empty hole that my father's legacy has left inside me.

Mya was right; there are still wolves in these woods. They were at risk of extinction in this area. Wolves need a lot of land to roam, and if that land gets smaller there's no room for competing packs.

I've stopped the land grab, and now the wolves are thriving. I've been monitoring them myself. They're beautiful creatures, wolves. Fierce hunters, but loyal to their pack and gentle to their mates, much simpler than humans.

The rumor is that I'm burning through my father's inheritance, spending it all on women and drugs. And they're half right. But I'm not spending it on what they think. I'm not as much of a womanizer as the rumors make me out to be, but I let them think what they like. I'm a wolf man. I'm working to preserve their habitat.

I reach Mya's place and bang on the door. There's no answer.

"Mya!" I try both front and back, but she's not in.

A neighbor comes out with a bag of trash. "You just missed her," she says.

"You know where she went?"

"No idea. Got in a taxi and drove off."

She must have gone to get her car. Why didn't she wake me? I would have given her a lift. I would have made her breakfast first and made love to her again. Slowly this time.

At least she got home safe. I head back to my place for a shower and breakfast. But I can't sit still.

I'm thinking about Mya and last night and how good it felt to fall asleep with her in my arms.

I go to my refuge, the woods. The silent trees are like old friends, and I wander through my favorite trails. I reach a stony ridge when the hairs on the back of my neck prickle. Looking down at me from the ridge is a grey wolf.

It's the one I've called Covey, a young female in the main pack. She's curious and often strays on her own. After a while she ducks her head and moves on. I turn around and head back home. I know I should give Mya some space, but I have to see her again.

I'm relieved to see her car's in the drive when I pull up.

I know something is wrong as soon as she opens the door. Her brow is creased, and her eyes are red like she's been crying.

"Brit's run away," she says.

I follow her into the house, and she leads me into a small living room.

"I've been to all her friends' houses, all the places she hangs out. But no one's seen her."

"Have you called the police?"

"I don't want to get them involved. They'll take her from me." She sinks into the sofa, and I stand in front of her.

"Why didn't you come to me?"

"Why would I come to you?"

"You don't have to be so independent, Mya,"

"I'm not being independent. You made it perfectly clear yesterday how this would go." She folds her arms

SADIE KING

and looks away. "That you'd fuck me and never think of me again. So why would I come to you for help?"

I pace the room, my fists clenching. I'm so angry at myself.

"Is that what you want?"

"No," she says. "But what do I know?"

"Oh, Mya, I said that to push you away. Because you deserve better than a man like me."

"But it's you that I want."

"And it's you that I want, Mya." I crouch down in front of her. "You make me feel like I could be somebody else, a better man."

"You're already a good man."

A warmth flows from my heart, and I take her hands in mine.

"Mya, I want to spend the rest of my life with you. You're the only woman for me." I press my lips gently to hers. "But first we need to find your sister."

"I've got no idea where she went."

"Leave it to me," I say. "You stay here, and I'll go find her."

Before she can protest, I'm out the door and into my car. If my hunch is right, I know exactly where Brit is.

The neon light flashes "girls, girls, girls." I grab my baseball cap from the glove box and pull it on. I'm not sure if Karl has banned me from all his strip joints, but I'm not taking the chance.

BEAST IN THE WOODS

I keep my eyes lowered, and the bouncer nods me in. It's a Friday afternoon, and the place is mostly empty. There's a couple of men drinking on their own and a few small groups. A woman dances slowly on the main stage; she looks bored, and I don't blame her. It's a dull crowd, and no one's paying her much attention.

I order a beer from the bar and take a seat in a booth where I can watch the room.

It doesn't take long for me to spot Brit. She's waitressing in little more than her underwear. Her long hair is tied back, and she swishes it seductively against her bare back. She's at a table of young men, smiling flirtatiously. One of them holds out a note, and she leans in to let him slip it down her bra. If Mya could see this, it would break her heart.

A waitress comes over to my table.

"Can I get you a beer, sugar?"

"I'd like a lap dance."

Her eyes soften. "Sure. Just let me deliver my next round of drinks, and I'll meet you in the private dance booth."

"With her," I say, indicating Brit.

The waitress's eyes harden.

"If that's what you want, fine. But I gotta tell you. She's new. She doesn't know the tricks like I do."

I look at her coldly. "Tell her to meet me in the dance booth. And here's something for your trouble."

I slip her a hundred, and she stuffs it down her bra. "She'll be there in five minutes."

SADIE KING

I saunter over to the lap dance area and pay my money.

"No touching and no soliciting," says the bouncer, ushering me in.

The gold beaded curtain swishes closed behind me, and I take a seat on the vinyl chair.

In a few minutes, the curtain parts and Brit appears.

"I hear you requested a..." She stops mid-sentence when she sees me, the coy smile sliding off her face. "What are you doing here?"

"I could ask you the same thing."

"Did Mya send you?"

"Mya doesn't know I'm here, and she doesn't know you're here either."

Relief spreads across her face.

"Why are you here, Brit?"

"To make money. I can do a shift here and earn twice as much as Mya gets in a week."

"So it's about the money?"

"Not just the money. Mya thinks she's the boss of me, but she isn't. She's a hypocrite. Always nagging me about my life choices and now here she is giving herself to the biggest player in town. I know she snuck out of the house last night. And I'm pretty fucking sure it was to spend the night with you."

"You ran away because you're angry at her?"

"Yes, I'm angry at her. For giving herself up to a man like you."

"I'm going to marry your sister."

Her mouth hangs open. "You're what?"

58

"I'm going to marry her and take care of her, if she'll let me."

For a moment Brit drops the tough girl act, and a look of stunned happiness sweeps across her face. "Mya's getting married?" She looks so much like her sister with a genuine smile on her face. Then it's gone. "What's in it for you? You're not the kind of guy who gets married."

"There's a lot you don't know about me, Brit. I'm in love with your sister, and if she consents to marry me, like it or not, we're going to be family. So get your bags. We're going home."

She looks at me in stunned silence.

"So now instead of Mya telling me what to do, I'll have both of you telling me what to do?"

"No." I shake my head. "You can do what you want. But I'm going to build a family with Mya, children, a future. I'd like you to be a part of that.

"But it will break your sister's heart to find out you're working in a place like this. Is that what you really want?"

She sits down next to me, and I can tell I'm getting through to her. I press on.

"You can come and live in the house with us if you want, or you can go away to college, or you can go traveling the world if that's what you really want. But we're family now, and I can't let you work in a place like this."

"You're a hypocrite too."

"Maybe. Or maybe I don't want you making the

SADIE KING

same mistakes I've made. I'm offering you another option."

She wraps her arms around her bare shoulders.

"You won't want me living in your house, cramping your style."

"You're Mya's family." I shrug. "You're all she has."

The bouncer pushes his head through the beaded curtain.

"Hey, less talking, more dancing."

Brit looks at me for a moment.

"Nah," she says, standing up. "I'm done with dancing."

She pushes her way past him. "Let's get out of here."

The bouncer advances on me, his brow furrowed. "Time to leave, buddy."

"With pleasure," I say.

I drive Brit back to Mya's.

"How did you know I was there?" she asks.

"I saw Karl slip you something at the party. When Mya said you'd run off, I guessed it was one of his cards. He owns half the clubs in town."

"I don't want to tell Mya where I went. She'll never forgive herself."

"I won't say anything if you don't want me to, but if she asks me directly, I won't lie to her."

Brit thinks about this for a moment. "Let's tell her you found me at Karl's place. It's half the truth. She doesn't have to know it was his strip club."

"Fine. But you pull a stunt like this again, and I'll lose all trust in you."

"Fine."

I pull up outside their house, and before the car stops Mya comes running out. She pulls Brit into an embrace, and they go inside the house. I don't want to interrupt their tearful reunion, so I leave them to it and drive home.

Later that night the buzzer to the gate rings. I check the security camera. It's Mya. I buzz the gate open and go out to meet her. There's a cold breeze, and I walk her to the house and into the warm kitchen.

"I came to say thank you," she says. "For bringing Brit home."

"I'm glad she came back," I say.

"So, she said some weird things." She's twisting her t-shirt nervously.

"Like what?" I say, enjoying seeing her squirm.

"Like we were all going to live together in this big house like one big happy family."

"Sounds nice."

"She had this crazy idea that we were getting married."

"Would that be so crazy?"

She laughs nervously, and I trap her hand in mine.

"I know we've only just met, but I've never felt so certain about anything in my life. You're the woman for me, Mya. I want you in my life forever."

SADIE KING

"I feel that too," she says. "Are we crazy?"

"Maybe," I say. "Marry me and we'll find out."

She gives me that big wide-eyed innocent look.

"Yes." She nods. "Yes, yes, yes! I'll marry you."

I scoop her into my arms and spin her around the kitchen, knocking a pan to the floor.

My heart is so full it might burst. I have the woman I love in my arms, and this big old house is starting to feel like it might be a home after all.

EPILOGUE

MYA

Six years later...

*T*he little girl steps in front of the group of children and glances cautiously behind at her teacher, who gives her a nod of encouragement.

"Thank you for showing us around the wolf place." The little girl hands me a piece of paper with a child's drawing of a wolf amongst the trees.

I recognize her as Carley Brookes the granddaughter of the notorious Damon Fletcher who once ruled the Sunset Coast but got soft when he became a granddaddy.

"That's a lovely picture, thank you."

I pin it on the chalk board and turn to the school group sitting around the low tables in the learning center.

"It's been lovely to meet you all. I hope you enjoyed the visit."

SADIE KING

"What do you say to Mrs. Bancroft?" says the teacher.

"Thank you, Mrs. Bancroft." The little voices speak in well-practiced unison.

"Thank you for coming. I hope you come back to see us next year."

I waddle over to the door, because I'm at the waddling stage of my pregnancy now, and head through to the main visitor center.

"For god's sake, sit down and rest, would you?" Brit's heels clack on the wooden floor as she rushes over to take my arm.

"I'm not an invalid," I say, waving her away.

She folds her arms across her tailored dress and raises an eyebrow at me. "If anything happened to you, Lucas would kill me. So sit down while I make some coffee, and that's decaf for you."

I roll my eyes, but I let her lead me into the office and gratefully sink into a chair.

We opened the visitor's center shortly after we were married. It now has over a million visitors a year and a lot of those are school groups. They come to walk the wooded trails and learn about the wolves that live in the area.

After graduating college, Brit came to work for us as our Chief Marketing Officer. You wouldn't recognize the confident young woman with her sharp bobbed haircut and tailored outfits. There's no sign of the rebellious teenager she once was.

I moved into the big house with Lucas, and it wasn't

long before we started filling it with our new family. We've got three children with another arriving very soon.

We're using the whole house now. We had to move the bats out of the empty rooms. They were re-homed beneath a rocky outcrop in the woods. We built the visitor's center near it, and visiting the bats is one of the highlights for school children.

We repaired the damage they'd done to the house and decorated the spare bedrooms. Now we open our home to visiting scientists and researchers who want to study the area and the animals. They stay for free, and we often sponsor the research.

Because of the work my husband did in preserving the woods, the wolf population in this area is thriving again. Bird populations are growing, and of course there are the bats. He's a good man, my husband.

Brit brings me the coffee, and we chat for a while about an upcoming fundraising ball we're organizing. The baby inside me kicks at my belly, reminding me not to make too many plans. I rub the protruding foot gently.

"Don't worry, little one, I'll miss the ball for you if I have to."

The door to the visitor's center bangs open, and Lucas strides in. His large frame means he almost has to duck to get through the door. He's been out in the woods all day with a group of researchers. His boots are muddy, there's dirt on his jeans, and his hair is windswept. I feel a rush of heat between my legs at the sight of him looking so rugged.

"Shouldn't you be at home resting?" He kisses me on the forehead and rubs my belly.

"How's our little man doing?"

"He's restless today."

"Must know it's a full moon tonight."

He helps me to my feet. "I'm going to get you home."

We wave goodbye to Brit, and he leads me to the car.

"I need you home and rested, Mya," he whispers as we leave. "I've got plans for you tonight."

A shiver of anticipation runs through my body.

We always go into the woods on a full moon. Once the kids are asleep, with the babysitter watching over them, we'll creep out of the house and across the dark lawn and into the cover of the trees.

There's something about the darkness, the woods, and the moonlight that release the beast inside my husband.

We'll find a sturdy tree or a pile of leaves and make love, urgent and needy and guided by our animal instincts.

With the moon full in the sky, we'll howl out our pleasure to the dark woods and listen to the sound echo back to us. Two animals, two lovers, joined by our need for each other and howling out our union.

WHAT TO READ NEXT

CONDUCTOR OF HEARTS

A curvy delivery girl with a talent and an older billionaire who's passion could be her undoing...

Ayden

I've returned home after years of travelling the world, but I'm getting restless and ready to move on. Then I find Laila sitting at my piano. The music fills my empty house, lifts my soul, and sets my body on fire. I'll do just about anything to keep her playing, and I'm beginning to realize some things are worth sticking around for.

Laila

I've worked hard to get an audition at a prestigious music school. But with two days to go I meet Ayden. Now my head's spinning, my body's in a fever, and I'm stumbling over the notes. Can I pull it together for the audition, or will this gorgeous, globe-trotting entrepreneur be my downfall?

Conductor of Hearts is a short and steamy age gap billionaire romance featuring an older man and a younger innocent woman.

GET YOUR FREE BOOK

Sign up to the Sadie King mailing list for a FREE book!

Fox in the Garden is an age gap steamy romance featuring an OTT billionaire and the younger woman he claims as his own.

It's a bonus book in the Filthy Rich Love series, exclusive to my email subscribers.

Sign up here:
authorsadieking.com/bonus-scenes

If you're already a subscriber check your latest email for the link that will take you to all the bonus content.

BOOKS & SERIES BY SADIE KING

Sunset Coast

Underground Crows MC

Short and steamy MC romance stories of obsessed men and curvy girls.

Sunset Security

A security firm run by ex-military men who become obsessed with their curvy girls.

Filthy Rich Love

The billionaires of the Sunset Coast. These alpha men fall hard and fall fast for the younger curvy women who crash into their world.

Men of the Sea

Super short and steamy tales from Temptation Bay of bad boys and curvy girls.

Love and Obsession

A bad boy trilogy featuring a thief, a henchman and an ex-military hitman who finds redemption with his curvy girl.

Wild Heart Mountain

Military Heroes

Kobe brings together a group of military veterans who live on the side of Wild Heart Mountain. Can these wounded warriors find love or do their scars cut too deep?

Wild Riders MC

This group of ex-military bikers fall hard and fall fast when they encounter the curvy women who heal their hearts.

Mountain Heroes

Steamy stories featuring the men and women from Wild Heart Mountain's Search and Rescue and Fire service.

Temptation

A damaged hero and a lost virgin in an explosive instalove retelling of the Hansel and Gretel story set in the woods of Wild Heart Mountain.

A Runaway Bride for Christmas

A snowstorm keeps this runaway bride trapped in the cabin of the mountain's biggest grump.

A Secret Baby for Christmas

Mr. Porter's Christmas takes a surprise turn when his daughter's best friend turns up with his baby.

Maple Springs

Small Town Sisters

Five curvy sister's inherit a dog hotel. But can they find love? Short and steamy instalove romance!

Candy's Café

A small-town cafe that's all heart. Meet the sister's who run it and the customer's who keep coming back.

All the Single Dads

These single dad hotties are fiercely protective and will do anything for the ones they love.

Men of Maple Mountain

These men are OTT possessive and will stop at nothing to claim the curvy innocent women they become obsessed with.

The Carter Family

Blue collar men find love with curvy girls in these quick read instalove romances.

Curvy Girls Can

Short, sweet and steamy instalove stories about sassy curvy women and the men who love them.

The Seal's Obsession

A soft stalker, secret baby, military romance. Featuring an OTT obsessed alpha male and a sassy curvy girl.

Kings County

Kings of Fire

Smoking hot tales of insta-love, featuring brave heroes and sassy heroines that will melt your heart.

King's Cops

Do you love police romance books? Then the King's Cops series is for you! Short, sweet and steamy tales of insta-love, featuring brave heroes and sassy heroines that will melt your heart.

For a full list of Sadie King's books check out her website

www.authorsadieking.com

ABOUT THE AUTHOR

Sadie King is a USA Today Best Selling Author of over 120 short and steamy contemporary romances. She loves writing about military heroes and the sassy women who heal their hearts.

Sadie lives in New Zealand with her ex-military husband and raucous young son.

When she's not writing she loves catching waves with her son, running along the beach, and drinking good wine, preferably with a book in hand.

www.authorsadieking.com

THANK YOU

Thank you for reading my story! If you enjoyed it, please consider leaving a review, they mean so much to authors and it helps other readers find books they might like.

Thank you!
Sadie xx

Milton Keynes UK
Ingram Content Group UK Ltd.
UKHW030900151124
451262UK00001B/23